THE THREE GOLDEN APPLES

A WONDER-BOOK FOR GIRLS AND BOYS

NATHANIEL HAWTHORNE

INTRODUCTORY TO "THE THREE GOLDEN APPLES"

The snow-storm lasted another day; but what became of it afterwards, I cannot possibly imagine. At any rate, it entirely cleared away, during the night; and when the sun arose, the next morning, it shone brightly down on as bleak a tract of hill-country, here in Berkshire, as could be seen anywhere in the world. The frost-work had so covered the windowpanes that it was hardly possible to get a glimpse at the scenery outside. But, while waiting for breakfast, the small populace of Tanglewood had scratched peepholes with their finger-nails, and saw with vast delight that—unless it were one or two bare patches on a precipitous hillside, or the gray effect of the snow, intermingled with the black pine forest—all nature was as white as a sheet. How exceedingly pleasant! And, to make it all the better, it was cold enough to nip one's nose short off! If people have but life enough in them to bear it, there is nothing that so raises the spirits, and makes the blood ripple and dance so nimbly, like a brook down the slope of a hill, as a bright, hard frost.

No sooner was breakfast over, than the whole party, well muffled in furs and woollens, floundered forth into the midst of the snow. Well, what a day of frosty sport was this! They slid down hill into the valley, a hundred times, nobody knows how far; and, to make it all the merrier, upsetting their sledges, and tumbling head over heels, quite as often as they came safely to the bottom. And, once, Eustace Bright took Periwinkle, Sweet Fern, and Squash-blossom, on the sledge with him, by way of insuring a safe passage; and down they went, full speed. But, behold, half-way down, the sledge hit against a hidden stump, and flung all four of its passengers into a heap; and, on gathering themselves up, there was no little Squash-blossom to be found! Why, what could have become of the child? And while they were wondering and staring about, up started Squash-blossom out of a snow-bank, with the reddest face you ever saw, and looking as if a large scarlet flower had suddenly sprouted up in midwinter. Then there was a great laugh.

When they had grown tired of sliding down hill, Eustace set the children to digging a cave in the biggest snow-drift that they could find. Unluckily, just as it was completed, and the party had squeezed themselves into the hollow, down came the roof upon their heads, and buried every soul of them alive! The next moment, up popped all their little heads out of the ruins, and the tall student's head in the midst of them, looking hoary and venerable with the snow-dust that had got amongst his brown curls. And then, to punish Cousin Eustace for advising them to dig such a tumble-down cavern, the children attacked him in a body, and so bepelted him with snowballs that he was fain to take to his heels.

So he ran away, and went into the woods, and thence to the margin of Shadow Brook, where he could hear the streamlet grumbling along, under great overhanging banks of snow and ice, which would scarcely let it see the light of day. There were adamantine icicles glittering around all its little cascades. Thence be strolled to the shore of the lake, and beheld a white, untrodden plain before him, stretching from his own feet to the foot of Monument Mountain. And, it being now almost sunset, Eustace thought that he had never beheld anything so fresh and beautiful as the scene. He was glad that the children were not with him; for their lively spirits and tumble-about activity would quite have chased away his higher and graver mood, so that he would merely have been merry (as he had already been, the whole day long), and would not have known the loveliness of the winter sunset among the hills.

When the sun was fairly down, our friend Eustace went home to eat his supper. After the meal was over, he betook himself to the study, with a purpose, I rather imagine, to write an ode, or two or three sonnets, or verses of some kind or other, in praise of the purple and golden clouds which he had seen around the setting sun. But, before he had hammered out the very first rhyme, the door opened, and Primrose and Periwinkle made their appearance.

"Go away, children! I can't be troubled with you now!" cried the student, looking over his shoulder, with the pen between his fingers. "What in the world do you want here? I thought you were all in bed!"

"Hear him, Periwinkle, trying to talk like a grown man!" said Primrose. "And he seems to forget that I am now thirteen years old, and may sit up almost as late as I please. But, Cousin Eustace, you must put off your airs, and come with us to the drawing-room. The children have talked so much about your stories, that my father wishes to hear one of them, in order to judge whether they are likely to do any mischief."

"Poh, poh, Primrose!" exclaimed the student, rather vexed. "I don't believe I can tell one of my stories in the presence of grown people. Besides, your father is a classical scholar; not that I am much afraid of his scholarship, neither, for I doubt not it is as rusty as an old case-knife, by this time. But then he will be sure to quarrel with the admirable nonsense that I put into these stories, out of my own head, and which makes the great charm of the matter for children, like yourself. No man of fifty, who has read the classical myths in his youth, can possibly understand my merit as a re-inventor and improver of them."

"All this may be very true," said Primrose, "but come you must! My father will not open his book, nor will mamma open the piano, till you have given us some of your nonsense, as you very correctly call it. So be a good boy, and come along."

Whatever he might pretend, the student was rather glad than otherwise, on second thoughts, to catch at the opportunity of proving to Mr. Pringle what an excellent faculty he had in modernizing the myths of ancient times. Until twenty years of age, a young man may, indeed, be rather bashful about showing his poetry and his prose; but, for all that, he is pretty apt to think that these very productions would place him at the tip-top of literature, if once they could be known. Accordingly, without much more resistance, Eustace suffered Primrose and Periwinkle to drag him into the drawing-room.

It was a large handsome apartment, with a semicircular window at one end, in the recess of which stood a marble copy of Greenough's Angel and Child. On one side of the fireplace there were many shelves of books, gravely but richly bound. The white light of the astrallamp, and the red glow of the bright coal-fire, made the room brilliant and cheerful; and before the fire, in a deep arm-chair, sat Mr. Pringle, looking just fit to be seated in such a chair, and in such a room. He was a tall and quite a handsome gentleman, with a bald brow; and was always so nicely dressed, that even Eustace Bright never liked to enter his presence, without at least pausing at the threshold to settle his shirt-collar. But now, as Primrose had hold of one of his hands, and Periwinkle of the other, he was forced to make his appearance with a rough-and-tumble sort of look, as if he had been rolling all day in a snow-bank. And so he had.

Mr. Pringle turned towards the student, benignly enough, but in a way that made him feel how uncombed and unbrushed he was, and how uncombed and unbrushed, likewise, were his mind and thoughts.

"Eustace," said Mr. Pringle, with a smile, "I find that you are producing a great sensation among the little public of Tanglewood, by the exercise of your gifts of narrative. Primrose here, as the little folks choose to call her, and the rest of the children, have been so loud in praise of your stories, that Mrs. Pringle and myself are really curious to hear a specimen. It would be so much the more gratifying to myself, as the stories appear to be an attempt to render the fables of classical antiquity into the idiom of modern fancy and feeling. At least, so I judge from a few of the incidents, which have come to me at second hand."

"You are not exactly the auditor that I should have chosen, sir," observed the student, "for fantasies of this nature."

"Possibly not," replied Mr. Pringle. "I suspect, however, that a young author's most useful critic is precisely the one whom he would be least apt to choose. Pray oblige me, therefore."

"Sympathy, methinks, should have some little share in the critic's qualifications," murmured Eustace Bright. "However, sir, if you will find patience, I will find stories. But be kind enough to remember that I am addressing myself to the imagination and sympathies of the children, not to your own."

Accordingly, the student snatched hold of the first theme which presented itself. It was suggested by a plate of apples that he happened to spy on the mantel-piece.

THE THREE GOLDEN APPLES.

Did you ever hear of the golden apples, that grew in the garden of the Hesperides? Ah, those were such apples as would bring a great price, by the bushel, if any of them could be found growing in the orchards of nowadays! But there is not, I suppose, a graft of that wonderful fruit on a single tree in the wide world. Not so much as a seed of those apples exists any longer.

And, even in the old, old, half-forgotten times, before the garden of the Hesperides was overrun with weeds, a great many people doubted whether there could be real trees that bore apples of solid gold upon their branches. All had heard of them, but nobody remembered to have seen any. Children, nevertheless, used to listen, open-mouthed, to stories of the golden apple-tree, and resolved to discover it, when they should be big enough. Adventurous young men, who desired to do a braver thing than any of their fellows, set out in quest of this fruit. Many of them returned no more; none of them brought back the apples. No wonder that they found it impossible to gather them! It is said that there was a dragon beneath the tree, with a hundred terrible heads, fifty of which were always on the watch, while the other fifty slept.

In my opinion it was hardly worth running so much risk for the sake of a solid golden apple. Had the apples been sweet, mellow, and juicy, indeed that would be another matter. There might then have been some sense in trying to get at them, in spite of the hundred-headed dragon.

But, as I have already told you, it was quite a common thing with young persons, when tired of too much peace and rest, to go in search of the garden of the Hesperides. And once the adventure was undertaken by a hero who had enjoyed very little peace or rest since he came into the world. At the time of which I am going to speak, he was wandering through the pleasant land of Italy, with a mighty club in his hand, and a bow and quiver slung across his shoulders. He was wrapt in the skin of the biggest and fiercest lion that ever had been seen, and which he himself had killed; and though, on the whole, he was kind, and generous, and noble, there was a good deal of the lion's fierceness in his heart. As he went on his way, he continually inquired whether that were the right road to the famous garden. But none of the country people knew anything about the matter, and many looked as if they would have laughed at the question, if the stranger had not carried so very big a club.

So he journeyed on and on, still making the same inquiry, until, at last, he came to the brink of a river where some beautiful young women sat twining wreaths of flowers.

"Can you tell me, pretty maidens," asked the stranger, "whether this is the right way to the garden of the Hesperides?"

The young women had been having a fine time together, weaving the flowers into wreaths, and crowning one another's heads. And there seemed to be a kind of magic in the touch of their fingers, that made the flowers more fresh and dewy, and of brighter lines, and sweeter fragrance, while they played with them, than even when they had been growing on their native stems. But, on hearing the stranger's question, they dropped all their flowers on the grass, and gazed at him with astonishment.

"The garden of the Hesperides!" cried one. "We thought mortals had been weary of seeking it, after so many disappointments. And pray, adventurous traveller, what do you want there?"

"A certain king, who is my cousin," replied he, "has ordered me to get him three of the golden apples."

"Most of the young men who go in quest of these apples," observed another of the damsels, "desire to obtain them for themselves, or to present them to some fair maiden whom they love. Do you, then, love this king, your cousin, so very much?"

"Perhaps not," replied the stranger, sighing. "He has often been severe and cruel to me. But it is my destiny to obey him."

"And do you know," asked the damsel who had first spoken, "that a terrible dragon, with a hundred heads, keeps watch under the golden apple-tree?"

"I know it well," answered the stranger, calmly. "But, from my cradle upwards, it has been my business, and almost my pastime, to deal with serpents and dragons."

The young women looked at his massive club, and at the shaggy lion's skin which he wore, and likewise at his heroic limbs and figure; and they whispered to each other that the stranger appeared to be one who might reasonably expect to perform deeds far beyond the might of other men. But, then, the dragon with a hundred heads! What mortal, even if he possessed a hundred lives, could hope to escape the fangs of such a monster? So kind-hearted were the maidens, that they could not bear to see this brave and, handsome traveller attempt what was so very dangerous, and devote himself, most probably, to become a meal for the dragon's hundred ravenous mouths.

"Go back," cried they all,—"go back to your own home! Your mother, beholding you safe and sound, will shed tears of joy; and what can she do more, should you win ever so great a victory? No matter for the golden apples! No matter for the king, your cruel cousin! We do not wish the dragon with the hundred heads to eat you up!"

The stranger seemed to grow impatient at these remonstrances. He carelessly lifted his mighty club, and let it fall upon a rock that lay half buried in the earth, near by. With the force of that idle blow, the great rock was shattered all to pieces. It cost the stranger no more effort to achieve this feat of a giant's strength than for one of the young maidens to touch her sister's rosy cheek with a flower.

"Do you not believe," said he, looking at the damsels with a smile, "that such a blow would have crushed one of the dragon's hundred heads?"

Then he sat down on the grass, and told them the story of his life, or as much of it as he could remember, from the day when he was first cradled in a warrior's brazen shield. While he lay there, two immense serpents came gliding over the floor, and opened their hideous jaws to devour him; and he, a baby of a few months old, had griped one of the fierce snakes in each of his little fists, and strangled them to death. When he was but a stripling, he had killed a huge lion, almost as big as the one whose vast and shaggy hide he now wore upon his shoulders. The next thing that he had done was to fight a battle with an ugly sort of monster, called a hydra, which had no less than nine heads, and exceedingly sharp teeth in every one of them.

"But the dragon of the Hesperides, you know," observed one of the damsels, "has a hundred heads!"

"Nevertheless," replied the stranger, "I would rather fight two such dragons than a single hydra. For, as fast as I cut off a head, two others grew in its place; and, besides, there was one of the heads that could not possibly be killed, but kept biting as fiercely as ever, long after it was cut off. So I was forced to bury it under a stone, where it is doubtless alive, to this vary day. But the hydra's body, and its eight other heads, will never do any further mischief."

The damsels, judging that the story was likely to last a good while, had been preparing a repast of bread and grapes, that the stranger might refresh himself in the intervals of his talk. They took pleasure in helping him to this simple food; and, now and then, one of them would put a sweet grape between her rosy lips, lest it should make him bashful to eat alone.

The traveller proceeded to tell how he had chased a very swift stag, for a twelve-month together, without ever stopping to take breath, and had at last caught it by the antlers, and carried it home alive. And he had fought with a very odd race of people, half horses and half men, and had put them all to death, from a sense of duty, in order that their ugly figures might never be seen any more. Besides all this, he took to himself great credit for having cleaned out a stable.

"Do you call that a wonderful exploit?" asked one of the young maidens, with a smile. "Any clown in the country has done as much!"

"Had it been an ordinary stable," replied the stranger, "I should not have mentioned it. But this was so gigantic a task that it would have taken me all my life to perform it, if I had not luckily thought of turning the channel of a river through the stable-door. That did the business in a very short time!"

Seeing how earnestly his fair auditors listened, he next told them how he had shot some monstrous birds, and had caught a wild bull alive, and let him go again, and had tamed a number of very wild horses, and had conquered Hippolyta, the warlike queen of the Amazons. He mentioned, likewise, that he had taken off Hippolyta's enchanted girdle, and had given it to the daughter of his cousin, the king.

"Was it the girdle of Venus," inquired the prettiest of the damsels, "which makes women beautiful?"

"No," answered the stranger. "It had formerly been the sword-belt of Mars; and it can only make the wearer valiant and courageous."

"An old sword-belt!" cried the damsel, tossing her head. "Then I should not care about having it!"

"You are right," said the stranger.

Going on with his wonderful narrative, he informed the maidens that as strange an adventure as ever happened was when he fought with Geryon, the six-legged man. This was a very odd and frightful sort of figure, as you may well believe. Any person, looking at his tracks in the sand or snow, would suppose that three sociable companions had been walking along together. On hearing his footsteps at, a little distance, it was no more than reasonable to judge that several people must be coming. But it was only the strange man Geryon clattering onward, with his six legs!

Six legs, and one gigantic body! Certainly, he must have been a very queer monster to look at; and, my stars, what a waste of shoe-leather!

When the stranger had finished the story of his adventures, he looked around at the attentive faces of the maidens.

"Perhaps you may have heard of me before," said he, modestly. "My name is Hercules!"

"We had already guessed it," replied the maidens; "for your wonderful deeds are known all over the world. We do not think it strange, any longer, that you should set out in quest of the golden apples of the Hesperides. Come, sisters, let us crown the hero with flowers!"

Then they flung beautiful wreaths over his stately head and mighty shoulders, so that the lion's skin was almost entirely covered with roses. They took possession of his ponderous club, and so entwined it about with the brightest, softest, and most fragrant blossoms, that not a finger's breadth of its oaken substance could be seen. It looked all like a huge bunch of flowers. Lastly, they joined hands, and danced around him, chanting words which became poetry of their own accord, and grew into a choral song, in honor of the illustrious Hercules.

And Hercules was rejoiced, as any other hero would have been, to know that these fair young girls had heard of the valiant deeds which it had cost him so much toil and danger to achieve. But, still, he was not satisfied. He could not think that what he had already done was worthy of so much honor, while there remained any bold or difficult adventure to be undertaken.

"Dear maidens," said he, when they paused to take breath, "now that you know my name, will you not tell me how I am to reach the garden of the Hesperides?"

"Ah! must you go so soon?" they exclaimed. "You—that have performed so many wonders, and spent such a toilsome life—cannot you content yourself to repose a little while on the margin of this peaceful river?"

Hercules shook his head.

"I must depart now," said he.

"We will then give you the best directions we can," replied the damsels. "You must go to the sea-shore, and find out the Old One, and compel him to inform you where the golden apples are to be found."

"The Old One!" repeated Hercules, laughing at this odd name. "And, pray, who may the Old One be?"

"Why, the Old Man of the Sea, to be sure!" answered one of the damsels. "He has fifty daughters, whom some people call very beautiful; but we do not think it proper to be acquainted with them, because they have sea-green hair, and taper away like fishes. You must talk with this Old Man of the Sea. He is a sea-faring person, and knows all about the garden of the Hesperides; for it is situated in an island which he is often in the habit of visiting."

Hercules then asked whereabouts the Old One was most likely to be met with. When the damsels had informed him, he thanked them for all their kindness,—for the bread and grapes with which they had fed him, the lovely flowers with which they had crowned him, and the songs and dances wherewith they had done him honor,—and he thanked them, most of all, for telling him the right way,—and immediately set forth upon his Journey.

But, before he was out of hearing, one of the maidens called after him.

"Keep fast hold of the Old-One, when you catch him!" cried she, smiling, and lifting her finger to make the caution more impressive. "Do not be astonished at anything that may happen. Only hold him fast, and he will tell you what you wish to know."

Hercules again thanked her, and pursued his way, while the maidens resumed their pleasant labor of making flower-wreaths. They talked about the hero, long after he was gone.

"We will crown him with the loveliest of our garlands," said they, "when he returns hither with the three golden apples, after slaying the dragon with a hundred heads."

Meanwhile, Hercules travelled constantly onward, over hill and dale, and through the solitary woods. Sometimes he swung his club aloft, and splintered a mighty oak with a downright blow. His mind was so full of the giants and monsters with whom it was the business of his life to fight, that perhaps he mistook the great tree for a giant or a monster. And so eager was Hercules to achieve what he had undertaken, that he almost regretted to have spent so much time with the damsels, wasting idle breath upon the story of his adventures. But thus it always is with persons who are destined to perform great things. What they have already done seems less than nothing. What they have taken in hand to do seems worth toil, danger, and life itself.

Persons who happened to be passing through the forest must have been affrighted to see him smite the trees with his great club. With but a single blow, the trunk was riven as by the stroke of lightning, and the broad boughs came rustling and crashing down.

Hastening forward, without ever pausing or looking behind, he by and by heard the sea roaring at a distance. At this sound, he increased his speed, and soon came to a beach, where the great surf-waves tumbled themselves upon the hard sand, in a long line of snowy foam. At one end of the beach, however, there was a pleasant spot, where some green shrubbery clambered up a cliff, making its rocky face look soft and beautiful. A carpet of verdant grass, largely intermixed with sweet-smelling clover, covered the narrow space between the bottom of the cliff and the sea. And what should Hercules espy there, but an old man, fast asleep!

But was it really and truly an old man? Certainly, at first sight, it looked very like one; but, on closer inspection, it rather seemed to be some kind of a creature that lived in the sea. For, on his legs and arms there were scales, such as fishes have; he was web-footed and web-fingered, after the fashion of a duck; and his long beard, being of a greenish tinge, had more the appearance of a tuft of sea-weed than of an ordinary beard. Have you never seen a stick of timber, that has been long tossed about by the waves, and has got all overgrown with barnacles, and, at last drifting ashore, seems to have been thrown up from the very deepest bottom of the sea? Well, the old man would have put you in mind of just such a wave-tost spar! But Hercules, the instant he set eyes on this strange figure, was convinced that it could be no other than the Old One, who was to direct him on his way.

Yes; it was the selfsame Old Man of the Sea, whom the hospitable maidens had talked to him about. Thanking his stars for the lucky accident of finding the old fellow asleep, Hercules stole on tiptoe towards him, and caught him by the arm and leg.

"Tell me," cried he, before the Old One was well awake, "which is the way to the garden of the Hesperides?"

As you may easily imagine, the Old Man of the Sea awoke in a fright. But his astonishment could hardly have been greater than was that of Hercules, the next moment. For, all of a sudden, the Old One seemed to disappear out of his grasp, and he found himself holding a stag by the fore and hind leg! But still he kept fast hold. Then the stag disappeared, and in its stead there was a sea-bird, fluttering and screaming, while Hercules clutched it by the wing and claw! But the bird could not get away. Immediately afterwards, there was an ugly three-headed dog, which growled and barked at Hercules, and snapped fiercely at the hands by which he held him! But Hercules would not let him go. In another minute, instead of the three-headed dog, what should appear but Geryon, the six-legged man-monster, kicking at Hercules with five of his legs, in order to get the remaining one at liberty! But Hercules held on. By and by, no Geryou was there, but a huge snake, like one of those which Hercules had strangled in his babyhood, only a hundred times as big, and it twisted and twined about the hero's neck and body, and threw its tail high into the air, and opened its deadly jaws as if to devour him outright; so that it was really a very terrible spectacle! But Hercules was no whit disheartened, and squeezed the great snake so tightly that he soon began to hiss with pain.

You must understand that the Old Man of the Sea, though he generally looked so much like the wave-beaten figure-head of a vessel, had the power of assuming any shape he pleased. When he found himself so roughly seized by Hercules, he had been in hopes of putting him into such surprise and terror, by these magical transformations, that the hero would be glad to let him go. If Hercules had relaxed his grasp, the Old One would certainly have plunged down to the very bottom of the sea, whence he would not soon have given himself the trouble of coming up, in order to answer any impertinent questions. Ninety-nine people out of a hundred, I suppose, would have been frightened out of their wits by the very first of his ugly shapes, and would have taken to their heels at once. For, one of the hardest things in this world is, to see the difference between real dangers and imaginary ones.

But, as Hercules held on so stubbornly, and only squeezed the Old One so much the tighter at every change of shape, and really put him to no small torture, he finally thought it best to reappear in his own figure. So there he was again, a fishy, scaly, webfooted sort of personage, with something like a tuft of sea-weed at his chin.

"Pray, what do you want with me?" cried the Old One, as soon as he could take breath; for it is quite a tiresome affair to go through so many false shapes. "Why do you squeeze me so hard? Let me go, this moment, or I shall begin to consider you an extremely uncivil person!"

"My name is Hercules!" roared the mighty stranger. "And you will never get out of my clutch, until you tell me the nearest way to the garden of the Hesperides!"

When the old fellow heard who it was that had caught him, he saw, with half an eye, that it would be necessary to tell him everything that he wanted to know. The Old One was an inhabitant of the sea, you must recollect, and roamed about everywhere, like other sea-faring people. Of course, he had often heard of the fame of Hercules, and of the wonderful things that he was constantly performing, in various parts of the earth, and how determined he always was to accomplish whatever he undertook. He therefore made no more attempts to escape, but told the hero how to find the garden of the Hesperides, and likewise warned him of many difficulties which must be overcome, before he could arrive thither.

"You must go on, thus and thus," said the Old Man of the Sea, after taking the points of the compass, "till you come in sight of a very tall giant, who holds the sky on his shoulders. And the giant, if he happens to be in the humor, will tell you exactly where the garden of the Hesperides lies."

"And if the giant happens not to be in the humor," remarked Hercules, balancing his club on the tip of his finger, "perhaps I shall find means to persuade him!"

Thanking the Old Man of the Sea, and begging his pardon for having squeezed him so roughly, the hero resumed his journey. He met with a great many strange adventures, which would be well worth your hearing, if I had leisure to narrate them as minutely as they deserve.

It was in this journey, if I mistake not, that he encountered a prodigious giant, who was so wonderfully contrived by nature, that, every time he touched the earth, he became ten times as strong as ever he had been before. His name was Antreus. You may see, plainly enough, that it was a very difficult business to fight with such a fellow; for, as often as he got a knock-down blow, up he started again, stronger, fiercer, and abler to use his weapons, than if his enemy had let him alone, Thus, the harder Hercules pounded the giant with his club, the further be seemed from winning the victory. I have sometimes argued with such people, but never fought with one. The only way in which Hercules found it possible to finish the battle, was by lifting Antaeus off his feet into the air, and squeezing, and squeezing, and squeezing him, until, finally, the strength was quite squeezed out of his enormous body.

When this affair was finished, Hercules continued his travels, and went to the land of Egypt, where he was taken prisoner, and would have been put to death, if he had not slain the king of the country, and made his escape. Passing through the deserts of Africa, and going as fast as he could, he arrived at last on the shore of the great ocean. And here, unless he could walk on the crests of the billows, it seemed as if his journey must needs be at an end.

Nothing was before him, save the foaming, dashing, measureless ocean. But, suddenly, as he looked towards the horizon, he saw something, a great way off, which he had not seen the moment before. It gleamed very brightly, almost as you may have beheld the round, golden disk of the sun, when it rises or sets over the edge of the world. It evidently drew nearer; for, at every instant, this wonderful object became larger and more lustrous. At length, it had come so nigh that Hercules discovered it to be an immense cup or bowl, made either of gold or burnished brass. How it had got afloat upon the sea, is more than I can tell you. There it was, at all events, rolling on the tumultuous billows, which tossed it up and down, and heaved their foamy tops against its sides, but without ever throwing their spray over the brim.

"I have seen many giants, in my time," thought Hercules, "but never one that would need to drink his wine out of a cup like this!"

And, true enough, what a cup it must have been! It was as large—as large—but, in short, I am afraid to say how immeasurably large it was. To speak within bounds, it was ten times larger than a great mill-wheel; and, all of metal as it was, it floated over the heaving surges more lightly than an acorn-cup adown the brook. The waves tumbled it onward, until it grazed against the shore, within a short distance of the spot where Hercules was standing.

As soon as this happened, he knew what was to be done; for he had not gone through so many remarkable adventures without learning pretty well how to conduct himself, whenever anything came to pass a little out of the common rule. It was just as clear as daylight that this marvellous cup had been set adrift by some unseen power, and guided hitherward, in order to carry Hercules across the sea, on his way to the garden of the Hesperides. Accordingly, without a moment's delay, he clambered over the brim, and slid down on the inside, where, spreading out his lion's skin, he proceeded to take a little repose. He had scarcely rested, until now, since he bade farewell to the damsels on the margin of the river. The waves dashed, with a pleasant and ringing sound, against the circumference of the hollow cup; it rocked lightly to and fro, and the motion was so soothing that, it speedily rocked Hercules into an agreeable slumber.

His nap had probably lasted a good while, when the cup chanced to graze against a rock, and, in consequence, immediately resounded and reverberated through its golden or brazen substance, a hundred times as loudly as ever you heard a church-bell. The noise awoke Hercules, who instantly started up and gazed around him, wondering whereabouts he was. He was not long in discovering that the cup had floated across a great part of the sea, and was approaching the shore of what seemed to be an island. And, on that island, what do you think he saw?

No; you will never guess it, not if you were to try fifty thousand times! It positively appears to me that this was the most marvellous spectacle that had ever been seen by Hercules, in the whole course of his wonderful travels and adventures. It was a greater marvel than the hydra with nine heads, which kept growing twice as fast as they were cut off; greater than the six-legged man-monster; greater than Antreus; greater than anything that was ever beheld by anybody, before or since the days of Hercules, or than anything that remains to be beheld, by travellers in all time to come. It was a giant!

But such an intolerably big giant! A giant as tall as a mountain; so vast a giant, that the clouds rested about his midst, like a girdle, and hung like a hoary beard from his chin, and flitted before his huge eyes, so that he could neither see Hercules nor the golden cup in which he was voyaging. And, most wonderful of all, the giant held up his great hands and appeared to support the sky, which, so far as Hercules could discern through the clouds, was resting upon his head! This does really seem almost too much to believe.

Meanwhile, the bright cup continued to float onward, and finally touched the strand. Just then a breeze wafted away the clouds from before the giant's visage, and Hercules beheld it, with all its enormous features; eyes each of them as big as yonder lake, a nose a mile Long, and a mouth of the same width. It was a countenance terrible from its enormity of size, but disconsolate and weary, even as you may see the faces of many people, nowadays, who are compelled to sustain burdens above their strength. What the sky was to the giant, such are the cares of earth to those who let themselves be weighed down by them. And whenever men undertake what is beyond the just measure of their abilities, they encounter precisely such a doom as had befallen this poor giant.

Poor fellow! He had evidently stood there a long while. An ancient forest had been growing and decaying around his feet; and oak-trees, of six or seven centuries old, had sprung from the acorn, and forced themselves between his toes.

The giant now looked down from the far height of his great eyes, and, perceiving Hercules, roared out, in a voice that resembled thunder, proceeding out of the cloud that had just flitted away from his face.

"Who are you, down at my feet there? And whence do you come, in that little cup?"

"I am Hercules!" thundered back the hero, in a voice pretty nearly or quite as loud as the giant's own. "And I am seeking for the garden of the Hesperides!"

"Ho! ho! ho!" roared the giant, in a fit of immense laughter. "That is a wise adventure, truly!"

"And why not?" cried Hercules, getting a little angry at the giant's mirth. "Do you think I am afraid of the dragon with a hundred heads!"

Just at this time, while they were talking together, some black clouds gathered about the giant's middle, and burst into a tremendous storm of thunder and lightning, causing such a pother that Hercules found it impossible to distinguish a word. Only the giant's immeasurable legs were to be seen, standing up into the obscurity of the tempest; and, now and then, a momentary glimpse of his whole figure, mantled in a volume of mist. He seemed to be speaking, most of the time; but his big, deep, rough voice chimed in with the reverberations of the thunder-claps, and rolled away over the hills, like them. Thus, by talking out of season, the foolish giant expended an incalculable quantity of breath, to no purpose; for the thunder spoke quite as intelligibly as he.

At last, the storm swept over, as suddenly as it had come. And there again was the clear sky, and the weary giant holding it up, and the pleasant sunshine beaming over his vast height, and illuminating it against the background of the sullen thunder-clouds. So far above the shower had been his head, that not a hair of it was moistened by the rain-drops!

When the giant could see Hercules still standing on the sea-shore, he roared out to him anew.

"I am Atlas, the mightiest giant in the world! And I hold the sky upon my head!"

"So I see," answered Hercules. "But, can you show me the way to the garden of the Hesperides?"

"What do you want there?" asked the giant.

"I want three of the golden apples," shouted Hercules, "for my cousin, the king."

"There is nobody but myself," quoth the giant, "that can go to the garden of the Hesperides, and gather the golden apples. If it were not for this little business of holding up the sky, I would make half a dozen steps across the sea, and get them for you."

"You are very kind," replied Hercules. "And cannot you rest the sky upon a mountain?"

"None of them are quite high enough," said Atlas, shaking his head. "But, if you were to take your stand on the summit of that nearest one, your head would be pretty nearly on a level with mine. You seem to be a fellow of some strength. What if you should take my burden on your shoulders, while I do your errand for you?"

Hercules, as you must be careful to remember, was a remarkably strong man; and though it certainly requires a great deal of muscular power to uphold the sky, yet, if any mortal could be supposed capable of such an exploit, he was the one. Nevertheless, it seemed so difficult an undertaking, that, for the first time in his life, he hesitated.

"Is the sky very heavy?" he inquired.

"Why, not particularly so, at first," answered the giant, shrugging his shoulders. "But it gets to be a little burdensome, after a thousand years!"

"And how long a time," asked the hero, "will it take you to get the golden apples?"

"O, that will be done in a few moments," cried Atlas. "I shall take ten or fifteen miles at a stride, and be at the garden and back again before your shoulders begin to ache."

"Well, then," answered Hercules, "I will climb the mountain behind you there, and relieve you of your burden."

The truth is, Hercules had a kind heart of his own, and considered that he should be doing the giant a favor, by allowing him this opportunity for a ramble. And, besides, he thought that it would be still more for his own glory, if he could boast of upholding the sky, than merely to do so ordinary a thing as to conquer a dragon with a hundred heads. Accordingly, without more words, the sky was shifted from the shoulders of Atlas, and placed upon those of Hercules.

When this was safely accomplished, the first thing that the giant did was to stretch himself; and you may imagine what a prodigious spectacle be was then. Next, he slowly lifted one of his feet out of the forest that had grown up around it; then, the other. Then, all at once, he began to caper, and leap, and dance, for joy at his freedom; flinging himself nobody knows how high into the air, and floundering down again with a shock that made the earth tremble. Then he laughed—Ho! ho! ho!—with a thunderous roar that was echoed from the mountains, far and near, as if they and the giant had been so many rejoicing brothers. When his joy had a little subsided, he stepped into the sea; ten miles at the first stride, which brought him mid-leg deep; and ten miles at the second, when the water came just above his knees; and ten miles more at the third, by which he was immersed nearly to his waist. This was the greatest depth of the sea.

Hercules watched the giant, as he still went onward; for it was really a wonderful sight, this immense human form, more than thirty miles off, half hidden in the ocean, but with his upper half as tall, and misty, and blue, as a distant mountain. At last the gigantic shape faded entirely out of view. And now Hercules began to consider what he should do, in case Atlas should be drowned in the sea, or if he were to be stung to death by the dragon with the hundred beads, which guarded the golden apples of the Hesperides. If any such misfortune were to happen, how could he ever get rid of the sky? And, by the by, its weight began already to be a little irksome to his head and shoulders.

"I really pity the poor giant," thought Hercules. "If it wearies me so much in ten minutes, how must it have wearied him in a thousand years!"

O my sweet little people, you have no idea what a weight there was in that same blue sky, which looks so soft and aerial above our heads! And there, too, was the bluster of the wind, and the chill and watery clouds, and the blazing sun, all taking their turns to make Hercules uncomfortable! He began to be afraid that the giant would never come back. He gazed wistfully at the world beneath him, and acknowledged to himself that it was a far happier kind of life to be a shepherd at the foot of a mountain, than to stand on its dizzy summit, and bear up the firmament with his might and main. For, of course, as you will easily understand, Hercules had an immense responsibility on his mind, as well as a weight on his head and shoulders. Why, if he did not stand perfectly still, and keep the sky immovable, the sun would perhaps be put ajar! Or, after nightfall, a great many of the stars might be loosened from their places, and shower down, like fiery rain, upon the people's heads! And how ashamed would the hero be, if, owing to his unsteadiness beneath its weight, the sky should crack, and show a great fissure quite across it!

I know not how long it was before, to his unspeakable joy, he beheld the huge shape of the giant, like a cloud, on the far-off edge of the sea. At his nearer approach, Atlas held up his hand, in which Hercules could perceive three magnificent golden apples, as big as pumpkins, all banging from one branch.

"I am glad to see you again," shouted Hercules, when the giant was within hearing. "So you have got the golden apples?"

"Certainly, certainly," answered Atlas; "and very fair apples they are. I took the finest that grew on the tree, I assure you. Ah! it is a beautiful spot, that garden of the Hesperides. Yes; and the dragon with a hundred heads is a sight worth any man's seeing. After all, you had better have gone for the apples yourself."

"No matter," replied Hercules. "You have had a pleasant ramble, and have done the business as well as I could. I heartily thank you for your trouble. And now, as I have a long way to go, and am rather in haste,—and as the king, my cousin, is anxious to receive the golden apples,—will you be kind enough to take the sky off my shoulders again?"

"Why, as to that," said the giant, chucking the golden apples into the air, twenty miles high, or thereabouts, and catching them as they came down,—"as to that, my good friend, I consider you a little unreasonable. Cannot I carry the golden apples to the king, your cousin, much quicker than you could? As his majesty is in such a hurry to get them, I promise you to take my longest strides. And, besides, I have no fancy for burdening myself with the sky, just now."

Here Hercules grew impatient, and gave a great shrug of his shoulders. It being now twilight, you might have seen two or three stars tumble out of their places. Everybody on earth looked upward in affright, thinking that the sky might be going to fall next.

"O, that will never do!" cried Giant Atlas, with a great roar of laughter. "I have not let fall so many stars within the last five centuries. By the time you have stood there as long as I did, you will begin to learn patience!"

"What!" shouted Hercules, very wrathfully, "do you intend to make me bear this burden forever?"

"We will see about that, one of these days," answered the giant. "At all events, you ought not to complain, if you have to bear it the next hundred years, or perhaps the next thousand. I bore it a good while longer, in spite of the back-ache. Well, then, after a thousand years, if I happen to feel in the mood, we may possibly shift about again. You are certainly a very strong man, and can never have a better opportunity to prove it. Posterity will talk of you, I warrant it!"

"Pish! a fig for its talk!" cried Hercules, with another hitch of his shoulders. "Just take the sky upon your head one instant, will you? I want to make a cushion of my lion's skin, for the weight to rest upon. It really chafes me, and will cause unnecessary inconvenience in so many centuries as I am to stand here."

"That's no more than fair, and I'll do it!" quoth the giant; for he had no unkind feeling towards Hercules, and was merely acting with a too selfish consideration of his own ease. "For just five minutes, then, I'll take back the sky. Only for five minutes, recollect!

I have no idea of spending another thousand years as I spent the last. Variety is the spice of life, say I."

Ah, the thick-witted old rogue of a giant! He threw down the golden apples, and received back the sky, from the head and shoulders of Hercules, upon his own, where it rightly belonged. And Hercules picked up the three golden apples, that were as big or bigger than pumpkins, and straightway set out on his journey homeward, without paying the slightest heed to the thundering tones of the giant, who bellowed after him to come back. Another forest sprang up around his feet, and grew ancient there; and again might be seen oak-trees, of six or seven centuries old, that had waxed thus again betwixt his enormous toes.

And there stands the giant, to this day; or, at any rate, there stands a mountain as tall as he, and which bears his name; and when the thunder rumples about its summit, we may imagine it to be the voice of Giant Atlas, bellowing after Hercules!

AFTER THE STORY.

"Cousin Eustace," demanded Sweet Fern, who had been sitting at the story-teller's feet, with his mouth wide open, "exactly how tall was this giant?"

"O Sweet Fern, Sweet Fern!" cried the student, "do you think I was there, to measure him with a yardstick? Well, if you must know to a hair's-breadth, I suppose he might be from three to fifteen miles straight upward, and that he might have seated himself on Taconic, and had Monument Mountain for a footstool."

"Dear me!" ejaculated the good little boy, with a contented sort of a grunt, "that was a giant, sure enough! And how long was his little finger?"

"As long as from Tanglewood to the lake," said Eustace.

"Sure enough, that was a giant!" repeated Sweet Fern, in an ecstasy at the precision of these measurements. "And how broad, I wonder, were the shoulders of Hercules?"

"That is what I have never been able to find out," answered the student. "But I think they must have been a great deal broader than mine, or than your father's, or than almost any shoulders which one sees nowadays."

"I wish," whispered Sweet Fern, with his mouth close to the student's ear, "that you would tell me how big were some of the oak-trees that grew between the giant's toes."

"They were bigger," said Eustace, "than the great chestnut-tree which stands beyond Captain Smith's house."

"Eustace," remarked Mr. Pringle, after some deliberation, "I find it impossible to express such an opinion of this story as will be likely to gratify, in the smallest degree, your pride of authorship. Pray let me advise you never more to meddle with a classical myth. Your imagination is altogether Gothic, and will inevitably Gothicize everything that you touch. The effect is like bedaubing a marble statue with paint. This giant, now! How can you have ventured to thrust his huge, disproportioned mass among the seemly outlines of Grecian fable, the tendency of which is to reduce even the extravagant within limits, by its pervading elegance?"

"I described the giant as he appeared to me," replied the student, rather piqued. "And, sir, if you would only bring your mind into such a relation with these fables as is necessary in order to remodel them, you would see at once that an old Greek had no more exclusive right to them than a modern Yankee has. They are the common property of the world, and of all time. The ancient poets remodelled them at pleasure, and held them plastic in their hands; and why should they not be plastic in my hands, as well?"

Mr. Pringle could not forbear a smile.

"And besides," continued Eustace, "the moment you put any warmth of heart, any passion or affection, any human or divine morality, into a classic mould, you make it quite another thing from what it was before. My own opinion is, that the Greeks, by taking possession of these legends (which were the immemorial birthright of mankind), and putting them into shapes of indestructible beauty, indeed, but cold and heartless, have done all subsequent ages an incalculable injury."

"Which you, doubtless, were born to remedy," said Mr. Pringle, laughing outright. "Well, well, go on; but take my advice, and never put any of your travesties on paper. And, as your next effort, what if you should try your hand on some one of the legends of Apollo?"

"Ah, sir, you propose it as an impossibility," observed the student, after a moment's meditation; "and, to be sure, at first thought, the idea of a Gothic Apollo strikes one rather ludicrously. But I will turn over your suggestion in my mind, and do not quite despair of success."

During the above discussion, the children (who understood not a word of it) had grown very sleepy, and were now sent off to bed. Their drowsy babble was heard, ascending the staircase, while a northwest-wind roared loudly among the tree-tops of Tanglewood, and played an anthem around the house. Eustace Bright went back to the study, and again endeavored to hammer out some verses, but fell asleep between two of the rhymes.